Wonder Kid Meets the Evil Lunch Snatcher

by Lois Duncan

Illustrated by Margaret Sanfilippo

Little, Brown and Company

Boston   New York   Toronto   London

Library of Congress Cataloging-in-Publication Data

Duncan, Lois, 1934 –
    Wonder Kid meets the evil lunch snatcher / by Lois Duncan.
    p. cm.
    Summary: Terrorized by an evil lunch-snatcher at his new
school, Brian devises, with the help of a fellow comic book fan, a
plan involving a new superhero called Wonder Kid.
    HC: ISBN 0-316-19558-8
    PB: ISBN 0-316-19561-8
    [1. Bullies — Fiction.   2. Moving, Household — Fiction.
3. Schools — Fiction.]   I. Title.
PZ7.D9117W0 1988
[E] — dc19   87-26490
                                                   CIP
                                                    AC

HC: 10 9 8 7 6 5 4 3 2
PB: 10 9 8 7

WOR

Published simultaneously in Canada
by Little, Brown & Company (Canada) Limited

Printed in the United States of America

Wond

the Evil

For Erin and Brittany Mahrer
with love

1

Right from the start Brian Johnson had known it would be a bad day.

Actually, it had been a bad month and a bad year. His father had lost his job and been offered another in a faraway town, so the Johnson family had been forced to move in the middle of the school year.

This particular day, though, started out wrong at breakfast. Brian was late to the table, and by the time he got there, his father was getting ready to go off to work, and his seven-year-old sister, Sarah, was cramming down the last of the sweet rolls. There was nothing left but cereal and cold toast.

Their mother was standing at the counter, making lunches.

"What on earth have you been doing so long?" she asked Brian.

"He was reading in the bathroom," said Sarah in a tattle-tale voice. "I know, because when I went in to brush my teeth I found one of his comic books on the floor."

"I don't know why you read that junk, Brian," their father said as he opened the door to leave. "With so many good books around, why do you waste your time on comics?"

"I don't know," Brian said. "I just sort of like them."

Actually, he *did* know why he liked to read old-time comic books. When a guy was shy

4

and skinny, it was comforting to imagine what it would be like to be a powerful superhero like Spiderman or Captain Marvel or Superman.

"You picked a bad time to get caught up in reading," his mother said. "Hurry up now and eat. You don't want to be late for your first day at your new school."

Brian sat down at the table in front of his bowl of cereal. Then he poured in milk. He ate a few bites and pushed the bowl away.

"I'm not very hungry," he said.

His mother set the lunches on the table.

"I know it's hard to eat when you're excited," she said.

"*I'm* excited, and *I* ate *my* breakfast," bragged Sarah. Sarah was always happy to gobble up anything.

"You and your brother are two different people," said their mother. She ruffled

Brian's hair in a loving way. "If you're sure you're finished, you and Sarah had better get going."

Brian slid out from under her hand and got up from the table.

He picked up his lunch sack. It was heavy. His mother always made good lunches.

His mother bent and kissed him. Then she kissed Sarah, leaving a red smudge on her cheek. Brian quickly wiped off his own cheek. The last thing he needed was to start his first day at Summerfield School smeared with lipstick.

"Have a happy day, kids," their mother said. "I know it's a little bit scary starting school in a new town, but think of all the wonderful friends you will make here! I'm sure in no time at all you will be having just as much fun at this new school as you did at your old one."

Her words kept ringing in Brian's ears after he and Sarah left the house. They made him feel sad and guilty. Just because he made the honor roll and his teachers said nice things about him, his parents thought he was well-adjusted and popular.

How disappointed they would be if they ever guessed the truth — that their son was a nerd.

7

Brian knew he would not make friends in Summerfield. He knew this because he hadn't had friends at his old school. The only people there who had even bothered to talk to him were a few wimpy kids who were nearly as nerdy as he was.

Summerfield School was only three blocks from the Johnson's new house. As he and Sarah walked toward it, Brian felt his stomach churning. He was glad his mother had not made him finish his breakfast.

The lower end of the school grounds was cut off from the street by a high hedge. Over the tips of the bushes, Brian could see the top of a swing set and the upper bars of a jungle gym.

There was a gateway cut in the hedge so people could walk through.

On the other side of the hedge a bell started ringing.

"We're late!" cried Sarah. "Oh, Brian, you made us late! You and your dumb old comics made us late our very first day!"

"I don't think we're *that* late," Brian said hopefully. "That's just the first bell. We'll still get to class on time."

"Well, hurry up!" snapped Sarah. "You're slow as a snail!"

She left his side and broke into a run.

Even though she was pudgy, his sister ran surprisingly fast. She went zipping through the opening in the hedge like a plump little bunny plunging into a rabbit hole.

"I told you, we're not going to be late!" Brian called after her. Then, beginning to feel worried, he too started to run.

He had almost reached the hole in the hedge when he heard Sarah scream.

"That's mine!" she shrieked. "You can't have that! Give it back!"

2

Brian raced through the opening in the hedge and burst out onto the playground.

What he saw there stopped him dead in his tracks.

Sarah was surrounded by a group of five tough-looking boys.

The largest of them had thick, black hair that stood up on his head in spikes. In his hand he was holding a brown paper sack.

"What are you doing with my sister's

lunch?" cried Brian. He wanted his voice to sound threatening, but it squeaked in a funny way.

"This isn't your sister's lunch anymore," said the boy. He opened the sack and began to rummage inside it. "Hey, look what a lot of stuff she has in here! Five chocolate chip cookies! That's one for each of us."

He took a bite of one cookie and tossed the others to his friends.

They all popped them into their mouths and started chewing.

"You robbers!" Sarah exploded. "Those cookies are mine!"

"I always like to eat dessert first," said the boy. "Now let's see what you've brought for my main course." He reached into the sack again and pulled more things out. "An apple, chips, and a sandwich. I wonder what kind it is." He unwrapped the sandwich and held it up to his nose. "Yuck! It smells like tuna. I can't stand tuna."

He dropped the sandwich onto the ground and put his foot on it.

The tuna filling squished out on both sides of his shoe.

Brian stared at the boy in disbelief.

"You can't do that!" he exclaimed. "You're wrecking her lunch!"

"That's a punishment for breaking the rules," said the boy.

"What rules?" cried Sarah. "I didn't do anything wrong!"

"You came through the Sixth-Grade Gate," the boy told her. "Only big kids are allowed to come in this entrance."

"I didn't know that," said Sarah. "The hedge didn't have a sign on it. Besides, that doesn't mean you can eat my cookies!"

The other four boys burst out laughing.

"You must be new here," one of them said. "Nobody tells Matt Gordon what he can't do. If Matt wants to eat cookies, Matt eats cookies."

"I'm going to tell!" Sarah shouted.

"No, you won't," said the boy named Matt. "Any kid who snitches on me is asking for trouble." He turned to Brian. "You came through the Sixth-Grade Gate too. That means I get two lunches instead of one."

"Don't you come near me!" said Brian, backing away.

"I'll do whatever I want!" Matt Gordon told him.

He lunged for Brian and grabbed the lunch sack out of his hand.

"Now, get out of here!" he commanded. "Be quick about it, too, or I'll step on your face just the way I stepped on that sandwich."

"Come on, Sarah," said Brian, grabbing his sister's hand.

He backed through the hole in the hedge, dragging Sarah with him.

I ought to be standing up to that creep, he thought miserably. The kids at my old school were right then they called me a wimp!

"So the lunch-snatcher gang got two new victims!" a voice said.

Brian spun around to find a boy watching him from the sidewalk. The boy had curly red hair and was wearing glasses.

"The other day I forgot and went in through that gate," he said. "Matt and his gang pulled my lunch apart and stamped on it."

"Why didn't you tell your teacher?" asked Sarah, blinking back tears. Sarah always hated to cry in front of strangers.

"Nobody snitches on Matt," the boy said bitterly. "Last year he picked on a first-grader, and she told her dad. He went to the principal, and Matt got detention. After that, he and his friends made that poor kid's life so miserable her folks had to put her in a private school."

Brian was so shocked he could hardly speak. "Can't *anybody* do *anything*? That guy's a *criminal!*"

The boy shook his head. "Matt runs the school. It would take a superhero to bring him to justice."

"It would take a . . . *what?*" Brian couldn't believe what he'd heard.

"A superhero," the boy repeated. "You know — like Batman. Or Plastic Man or Wonder Woman or — "

He broke off suddenly as though he were

afraid Brian would make fun of him.

"Or Captain Marvel," said Brian. "Or Spiderman or Superman."

The red-haired boy stared at him in astonishment.

"Do you read comic books too?"

"I have a whole collection," said Brian. "My dad calls them junk, but I feel good when I read them."

"I know. They make you feel powerful," the boy said, nodding. "My name's Robbie Chandler. I'm in fourth grade."

"I'm Brian Johnson," said Brian. "I'm in fourth grade too."

From behind the hedge, there came the sound of the bell again.

"That's the second bell!" shrieked Sarah. "Now we're *really* late!"

"We're late," agreed Robbie. "But we're all of us late together."

All of a sudden Brian found himself feeling much better.

16

3

The fourth-grade classroom at Summer-field School was not much different from the fourth-grade classroom back at Brian's old school. The desks were arranged the same way, and the big hand on the wall clock jumped from minute to minute with the same sharp clicking sound as the clock on the wall of his old classroom.

The two rooms even smelled the same, like chewing gum and tennis shoes and chalk dust.

And peanut butter.

And chocolate cake.

And bananas.

As the morning passed and the sack lunches that were stored in the cubbies at the back of the classroom got warmer and riper, Brian became more and more hungry. By the time twelve o'clock rolled around, his stomach was growling so loudly it sounded like a caged tiger.

"Whenever you children are finished eating you can go out and play," said their teacher, Mrs. Busby.

Brian felt sure he was going to like Mrs. Busby. She had kind eyes and a voice with a smile in it, and even though it was only his first day at Summerfield, she already knew his name.

"Didn't you bring a lunch, Brian?" she asked him.

For a moment Brian considered telling her what had happened to his lunch. Then he remembered Matt Gordon's words: "Any kid who snitches on me is asking for trouble."

There was no way he wanted trouble from Matt and his buddies.

"I did bring a lunch," he said. "I'm just not hungry."

Since he had nothing to eat, he got up and went outside. The playground was crowded with children. He glanced about him, feeling left out and lonely, the way he had often felt back at his old school.

At least he did not see Matt Gordon and his friends. Sixth-graders must have a later recess, he thought.

Suddenly he caught sight of his sister sitting on a bench. She was jabbering away at a girl with bright red hair.

Brian walked over to where the two girls were sitting. When he reached them he saw that they were eating potato chips.

"Hi," said Sarah. "This is Lisa, Robbie Chandler's sister. She's in third grade, and she's sharing her lunch with me. Lisa, this is my brother, Brian."

"Sarah told me what happened this morning," said Lisa. "I know what it's like to be jumped by Matt and his gang. On my birthday my mother baked cupcakes for all the kids in my class. The minute I came through the gate, Matt grabbed the box away."

"Hey, Brian!" Robbie's voice rang out across the playground.

Brian turned and saw his new friend hurrying toward them.

"You took off so fast, I couldn't catch up with you," Robbie said. He thrust a half of a sandwich into Brian's hand. "I hope you like cheese and tomato. That's all my mom packed today."

"Gee, thanks," said Brian, who would happily have eaten *anything*. He wolfed down

the sandwich so quickly he didn't even taste it.

"We were talking about that awful Matt," said Sarah. "I wish somebody would teach that bully a lesson."

"Like a superhero, maybe?" Robbie said, laughing. "It's too bad those powerful guys aren't real."

"Nobody has ever *proved* they aren't real," said Brian.

"Oh, come on!" exclaimed Sarah. "You know they're made up!"

"But what if they weren't?" said Brian. "Who would ever know it? Superheroes go around disguised as ordinary people. It's only when they're fighting evil that they put on their masks and costumes and start flying and jumping over buildings and zapping criminals."

"Sometimes they don't even have to zap criminals," said Robbie. "Sometimes the bad guys just get so scared they surrender."

Brian said, "I bet Matt would think twice about robbing people if he thought a super-hero was out to get him."

"He would never believe that," said Sarah.

"Most people believe what they read in the paper," said Lisa. She seemed to be thinking hard as she munched her potato chips. "It's possible Matt might believe a newspaper story, especially if there was a picture that went along with it."

"How could we get a story like that in the paper?" asked Sarah.

"Lisa could do it!" said Robbie. "She's a reporter for our school paper. She's always writing stories about interesting people."

"But the picture?" said Sarah. "Who would pose for that?"

"I would!" Brian said excitedly. "I could dress up in that Superman costume I wore on Halloween! Nobody could tell who it was if I wore a mask!"

"I wore a Spiderman costume last Halloween," said Robbie. "We could use the hood from that to cover up your hair."

Sarah regarded the two boys doubtfully. "Aren't superheroes big?"

"Not when they're young," said Brian. "Everybody starts out as a kid."

"I'd need help writing the story," Lisa told them. "I don't know much about how superheroes do things."

"No problem!" Robbie said with a grin. "Brian and I are experts! We'll come up with a story that will knock Matt Gordon's socks off!"

4

The paper with Lisa's article came out the next Monday.

By noon, the issue had sold out.

By the following day, even students who had not purchased the paper had read the copies their friends had bought, and everybody was talking about the superhero story.

Sarah felt very proud because she was in

it. She kept the article in her desk and read it over and over:

Sarah Johnson is a new second-grade student at Summerfield School. She says she likes it at Summerfield, but she misses her good friend Wonder Kid, who was a classmate at her old school.

"Wonder Kid is a superhero," says Sarah. "He rights wrongs. He protects the innocent. He leaps tall buildings with a single bound. He zaps criminals, especially lunch snatchers."

Sarah says Wonder Kid often flies here to visit her.

"Once a friend, always a friend," says Sarah.

Next to the story there was a snapshot of a boy wearing a cape and a mask. On the front of his shirt was a big letter W. The boy's arms were bulging with muscles.

He was pointing a finger at the camera.
The caption under the picture read: "*Criminals better shape up! Wonder Kid zaps!*"

By the end of the third day, Sarah had read the story so many times she was even beginning to imagine it was true.

"Look how strong Wonder Kid's arms are!" she said.

"Are you nuts?" Brian snorted. "You were there when we made those muscles. They're nothing but Mother's panty hose all bunched up."

"I know," Sarah sighed, "but they really do look awesome."

She was starting to like the thought of having a friend like Wonder Kid.

A lot of people seemed to believe the story, especially kids who watched a lot of television.

There were others, however, who did not take it seriously. Lisa's teacher complimented her on writing "such a cute little piece of fiction," and the kids in her enriched science class thought it was a joke.

"The only thing that counts is what Matt

thinks," said Robbie. "We can't blow our scheme by asking him, so we'll have to run a test."

"What sort of test?" asked Brian.

"Sarah will have to go through the Sixth-Grade Gate again," said Robbie. "If Matt and his gang don't jump her, we'll know they're scared."

Sarah did not like that idea one bit.

"It's not fair!" she said. "I don't want my lunch to be snatched again!"

"Let's take a vote," said Brian. "All in favor of running this test, raise your hand . . . "

The vote came out three to one in favor of the test.

Unable to argue further, Sarah gave in.

When she walked through the hole in the hedge, Matt was right there waiting.

"Look who's here!" he crowed. "The lunch-delivery girl!" With one quick grab, he had Sarah's sack in his hand.

"You give that back, or I'm going to call Wonder Kid!" Sarah shrieked.

"I don't believe that stupid story," Matt told her. "If Wonder Kid is your buddy, where are you keeping him?"

Sarah did not stop to think before she spoke. "You'll see him tomorrow!" she cried. "He's coming to visit! I've told him about how you lunch snatchers pick on people. He's coming to take revenge and protect his friends!"

"That's a crock of lies," said Matt, but he sounded uncertain.

He tossed Sarah's lunch sack back to the boy behind him.

"You can have this," he said. "It's probably tuna sandwiches."

"I don't want it," his friend said quickly. "I ate a big breakfast."

"I won't believe in this superdude till I've seen him," Matt told Sarah. "Bring him here to meet me tomorrow morning."

30

Sarah suddenly realized she had gone too far.

"He can't come tomorrow," she said. "Tomorrow's a school day."

"Wonder Kid goes to school!" Matt exclaimed in amazement. "Why would a superhero waste time in a classroom?"

"He doesn't think it's a waste of time," said Sarah. "Wonder Kid believes in education." She tried to remember the exact words her brother had used earlier. "Superheroes spend most of their time disguised as ordinary people. Wonder Kid goes to school like any other kid."

"Okay," said Matt. "You can bring him here after school then. But tell him he'd better be ready to show off his zapping."

5

"How could you have agreed to such a thing!" Brian exploded.

"I didn't know how to get out of it," said Sarah.

"So, what's the problem?" asked Robbie. "Why *can't* Matt meet Wonder Kid? All Brian has to do is put on his superhero costume."

"Matt doesn't want to *meet* Wonder Kid," said Brian. "What he wants is to see Wonder Kid in action."

"Then Wonder Kid can zap somebody," said Robbie. "That shouldn't be too hard to arrange. My grandfather gave me a magic set last Christmas. The wand has a battery in it that shoots off sparks."

"And we've got smoke bombs left over from Fourth of July," Lisa reminded him. "Remember how it rained so we couldn't shoot them off? Wonder Kid can appear in a cloud of smoke!"

Everybody was getting excited except Brian.

"If I zap Matt, and he doesn't feel it, he'll know Wonder Kid's a fake," he said.

"Then don't zap Matt," said Robbie. "Zap somebody else."

"Let's take a vote like we did before," suggested Sarah. "Everybody in favor of having Matt meet Wonder Kid, raise your hand."

The vote came out three to one in favor of the meeting.

Brian's stomach lurched in exactly the way

it had on his first day at the new school. Maybe he was getting the flu, he told himself hopefully.

The next morning he did wake up feeling sick, but not sick enough.

"You don't have a temp," said his mother, feeling his forehead. "I think it will be all right for you to go to school today."

Robbie had worked out the plan the evening before. Brian was to take his superhero costume and raincoat to school in his bookbag. He would store the bag in his cubby, and as soon as school let out, he would take it into the boys' room and change into Wonder Kid.

Then he would put his raincoat on over his costume.

Brian felt more and more nervous as the day went on. No matter how hard he tried, he could not keep his mind on his schoolwork.

Mrs. Busby had to call his name three times when it was his turn to do the times tables, and even then he couldn't remember the sixes.

Mrs. Busby looked worried.

"Brian, are you feeling all right?" she asked. "You got every one of your number facts right on yesterday's quiz. I can't believe you've forgotten the sixes already."

"I'm fine," said Brian, and wished that it were not true. He would have been much happier if he had been sent to the nurse's office.

The minute hand on the wall clock kept zipping along so fast that the day seemed to pass like a shot. When it made its final click into place and the bell rang to signal that school was out, Brian knew the moment he had been dreading had come at last.

He got up from his desk and walked slowly back to his cubby.

Robbie clapped him on the shoulder as he went by.

"Don't look so worried," he said. "We can pull it off."

"What do you mean, 'we'?" Brian snapped. "*I'm* the one who has to go out there with that dumb costume on."

"Stop making such a big deal out of this," said Robbie. "You seemed to like the costume when you wore it for the picture."

"Well, I don't like it now," said Brian. "This is a dumb idea."

Brian got his bookbag out of his cubby and took it with him into the boys' room. To his relief, nobody else was in there.

He went into one of the stalls and changed into all of the costume except the Spiderman hood. The big yellow *W* that Lisa had sewed onto the Superman shirt was beginning to come loose, so he stuck it back down with a glue stick he'd borrowed from art class.

Then he took his mother's panty hose out of the bookbag and wadded it up and stuffed it into his shirt. The bunched-up hose had looked like muscles in the photograph. He hoped it would still look that way on the playground.

When Brian left the rest room, the janitor was standing out in the hall, emptying waste-paper baskets into a trash cart.

He looked surprised when he saw Brian in his raincoat.

"You must know something I don't," he said. "Last time I looked out the window, the sun was shining."

"You never can tell when it might start raining," said Brian. "Storms can come up pretty fast this time of year."

He walked down the hall and out of the school building. Sarah was waiting outside the door with a grocery sack. In the sack there were smoke bombs, a box of matches, and a long black wand.

"Where are Robbie and Lisa?" Brian asked his sister.

"Out on the playground behind the school,"
said Sarah.

She looked as excited as if she were going
to a party.

"Let's hurry!" she squealed. "I can't wait
to see Matt's face when he finally gets his
chance to see Wonder Kid in action!"

6

Sarah continued to chatter like a happy little parrot as they walked along the sidewalk at the end of the school grounds.

Brian was too nervous to listen to her. He kept glancing at the hedge that cut off their view of the playground and wondering if Matt and his gang were behind it.

They stopped just short of the Sixth-Grade Gate so Brian could change the rest of the way into Wonder Kid.

He took the Spiderman hood out of his

bookbag and pulled it on over his head. Then he took off his raincoat.

A car passed by, and the driver turned around to stare at him. He looked as though he couldn't believe what he was seeing.

Brian's stomach did a flip-flop.

"I think I'm going to throw up," he said.

"Superheroes never throw up," said Sarah.

She opened the grocery sack and took out Robbie's wand. Brian took it from her and shoved it up his sleeve.

"Maybe Matt and his friends have forgotten to come," he said.

"I bet they haven't," said Sarah. "I'll check and see."

She dashed through the hole in the hedge and out onto the playground.

"They're here, all right!" she shouted back over her shoulder.

"Of course, we're here." Matt's voice sounded meaner than ever. "I see you're all by yourself. Where is your superbuddy?"

"He's coming," said Sarah. "He'll be along any minute now."

More than anything in the world, Brian wanted to run. Their house was only a couple of blocks away. In minutes he could be safely home with the door locked.

But that would mean leaving his sister alone with the lunch snatchers. He knew there was no way he could do that to Sarah.

He took the matches and a smoke bomb out of the grocery sack. He could not bend his right arm because of the wand, so he had to strike the match with his arms straight in front of him.

The matchstick snapped in two.

"Wonder Kid will be along any minute now," Sarah repeated loudly.

She paused a moment, and then she said it a third time.

Frantically, Brian yanked out another match

and struck it. This time the stick did not break, and the match burst into flame. With a gasp of relief, Brian held the flame to the wick of the smoke bomb. The bomb started to fizzle.

"This is it," Brian whispered. There was no turning back now. Crazy as the scheme might be, he had to go through with it.

Since he couldn't pitch with his stiff right arm, he took the bomb in his left hand and awkwardly tossed it in through the hole in the hedge. Then, before he could panic, he stepped through after it.

Thick, black smoke came billowing up all around him. He felt as though he were popping out through a cloud.

He heard a series of gasps from Matt and his friends.

All of a sudden, Brian didn't feel like a nerd anymore.

He felt like a guy who was able to leap tall buildings!

He felt like a hero who could bring evil criminals to justice!

"Do not fear! Wonder Kid's here!" he shouted. His voice rang out as powerful and strong as a superhero's.

"Here he is!" cried Sarah. "I knew my friend wouldn't fail me!"

Matt's buddies, who had been grouped around him, backed hastily away.

"I've got to get going," one said. "I've got homework to do."

"So do I," said another. "I have to study for a math quiz."

"Hey, what's with you guys?" exclaimed Matt. "Can't you see this guy's a fake? He doesn't have magic powers, and he isn't any superhero."

"He is, and he'll prove it!" cried Sarah. "Just wait till he zaps you!"

"He doesn't have to zap *me*," Matt said a bit nervously. "If he wants to zap somebody else, though, I don't mind watching."

"I really do need to go home now," said one of his friends.

"Don't be a coward," said Matt. "Stick around for the show."

"I never zap innocent people," Brian told them. "I'll prove my powers by zapping the roof off the school."

He raised his right arm and pointed his finger at the school. With his thumb, he pressed the switch on the wand from Robbie's magic set. The wand burst forth with a rattle like a machine gun, and a shower of sparks came shooting out of its tip.

The school did not seem to be injured, but a red-haired boy on the steps let out a terrible shriek and fell to the ground.

The girl who was standing next to him screamed in terror.

"My brother's been zapped!" Lisa cried. "Somebody call an ambulance!"

"I aimed too low," said Brian. "I'll try it
again."

Once more he raised his arm and pointed
his finger.

This time there was no one but Sarah to
see what happened. Matt and his friends were
halfway across the school yard.

7

The next issue of the school paper carried a banner headline: "SUMMERFIELD STUDENT ZAPPED BY SUPERHERO." The article read:

> Robbie Chandler, a fourth-grade student at Summerfield School, was zapped on the playground last Tuesday.
>
> The zapper was the well-known superhero Wonder Kid.
>
> Sarah Johnson, who witnessed the

zapping, said it was an accident.

"Wonder Kid did not mean to zap Robbie," she said. "Smoke got in his eyes, and his aim was off."

Matt Gordon and his gang were witnesses too, but they got scared and ran away.

Next to the article there was a picture of Robbie with a bandage around his head. The caption said, "*Victim of tragic zapping accident.*"

The paper sold out so fast a second edition had to be printed. Lisa was excused from class to help run the copy machine.

When school let out, Sarah found Matt Gordon and his gang waiting for her in the hall outside the second-grade classroom.

"Why did you tell that reporter we're scared of Wonder Kid?" Matt demanded. He looked and sounded furious.

"Because you are," said Sarah, trying not

to seem frightened. "As soon as you saw him zap Robbie, you turned and ran."

"I didn't run because I was scared," said Matt. "I ran because I thought I heard my mother calling. My friends and I think this Wonder Kid dude is a fake. We want to see him leap a tall building with a single bound."

"He's not free this afternoon," said Sarah. "He has to go to the dentist."

"Then he'd better be here first thing in the morning," Matt told her. "If we don't see Wonder Kid leap over a building, his 'good friend Sarah' won't be eating lunch for a year."

He screwed up his face into a horrible monster snarl. Behind him, all his gang members did the same thing. Sarah had never imagined they could look so awful.

"Oh, dear! I think I forgot my homework!" she said.

She rushed back into the classroom and slammed the door. It was ten whole minutes before she felt brave enough to open it again.

Finally she pulled it open just a crack and peeked out.

Matt and his friends were gone.

Sarah raced out of the room and down the hall. She zipped out of the building and ran at top speed all the way home.

Brian, Robbie, and Lisa were gathered in the Johnsons' front yard. They all had copies of the school paper and were taking turns reading Lisa's article out loud. They turned in surprise when Sarah came panting up to them.

"Where were you?" Lisa asked her. "I thought we were going to walk home from school together."

"Matt and his gang stopped me in the hall," explained Sarah. "Tomorrow morning they want to see Wonder Kid leap a building."

"There's no way Wonder Kid is going to do that," said Brian.

"But he has to!" cried Sarah. "If he doesn't, Matt will take away all my lunches for a year!"

Just thinking about it made her stomach growl with hunger.

"You know Wonder Kid can't jump over a building," said Brian. "You can't have forgotten his muscles are only panty hose."

There was a moment of silence.

Then Robbie said thoughtfully, "It's true that Wonder Kid can't jump over a building, but he might be able to make it over a hedge."

"That hedge by the playground? You've got to be kidding!" said Brian.

"We could set up a ladder behind the hedge," said Robbie. "If Wonder Kid jumped off that, he would land in the playground."

"Dad's stepladder is stored in our garage," said Lisa. "We could set that up on the sidewalk outside the Sixth-Grade Gate."

"I don't want to jump off a ladder," Brian said definitely.

"Let's vote," said Sarah. "Everybody in favor, raise your hand!"

Three hands shot up. Brian's hands went into his pockets.

"I won't do it," he said. "I won't jump off a ladder."

"Just think what a marvelous story it will make!" exclaimed Lisa. "I'm going to rush home right now and put film in the camera."

Brian said, "If I jump off a ladder, I'll break my legs."

"No, you won't," said Robbie. "We'll dig up the ground on the other side of the hedge. That way Wonder Kid will have a soft spot to land." He smiled his bright, sunny smile. He didn't seem worried at all.

"We'll hold a rehearsal first thing in the morning," he said.

8

The rehearsal was set for seven o'clock the next morning.

Brian had a hard time getting to sleep that night.

When his mother and father passed by his door on their way to their own room, he was still wide awake, trying not to think about tomorrow.

He did not want to jump off a ladder.

He did not want to leap over the top of a hedge.

Most of all, he did not want to have to face Matt Gordon and his gang again.

At some point during the night he must have fallen asleep, however, because suddenly to his surprise he felt somebody shaking him.

When he opened his eyes, the room was filled with the pale gray light of morning, and Sarah was standing next to his bed with her hand on his shoulder.

"We'd better get going," she said. "It's almost seven."

She looked excited and bright-eyed and well rested.

Brian got out of bed and put on his clothes. Then he packed his superhero costume into his bookbag again. Robbie had suggested that he change into the Wonder Kid outfit at the Chandlers' house since it was right across the street from the school.

When Brian and Sarah went downstairs, their mother was already in the kitchen making coffee.

"Where do you two think you're going?" she asked them.

"We have to get to school early today," said Sarah. "We promised to meet some people on the playground."

"You can't go to school without breakfast," their mother said firmly. She poured each of them a bowl of cereal.

Sarah wolfed hers down in half a minute. Brian put a spoonful of cereal into his mouth. He started to chew it.

"Hurry up," whispered Sarah. "We're already running late."

Brian tried to swallow. The cereal would not go down.

"I can't eat when I'm nervous," he whispered back.

Their mother was standing with her back toward them, making peanut butter sandwiches.

Quickly, Sarah stuck her own spoon into Brian's bowl and started shoveling cereal into her mouth.

Their mother got some apples out of the

refrigerator. Then she took a cake out of the cake box and cut two big slices.

Sarah gobbled faster.

By the time their mother had wrapped the cake and sandwiches and put those, along with the apples, into lunch sacks, there was nothing left in either Sarah's bowl or Brian's.

"Can we go now?" Sarah asked eagerly.

"I guess so," their mother said, staring down at the empty bowls. "You certainly must have been very hungry this morning."

Out in the front yard, Brian spat his mouthful of cereal into a rose bush. Then he and Sarah walked hurriedly over to the school grounds.

Robbie and Lisa were there ahead of them. They looked as if they had been waiting for quite a while.

"What took you so long?" asked Robbie. "Lisa and I have been here for ages. We've already brought the ladder over and spaded up the landing field."

The stepladder was set up outside the Sixth-Grade Gate. On it there hung a sign:

DANGER — HEDGE TRIMMERS AT WORK

A pair of clippers lay at the base of the ladder.

".The sign and clippers were my idea," said Lisa. "This way people won't wonder why there's a ladder on the sidewalk."

"You'd better hurry if you want a test jump," Robbie said to Brian. "If we wait any longer, Matt and his gang will be here."

Brian looked at the stepladder. It was a high one. It reached to the very top of the hedge.

Sarah could tell exactly what he was thinking.

"We voted," she reminded him. "It came out three to one in favor."

"I know," said Brian, "but I still don't think this is fair."

He handed his lunch sack to Sarah and placed one foot on the lowest rung of the ladder. Then he stepped up onto the second rung.

"It's shaky," he said. "I think it's going to fall over."

"No, it's not," said Robbie. "It's very well balanced."

Brian slowly climbed to the top of the ladder.

He gazed out across the hedge and then down to the playground below.

"The hedge is too wide," he said. "I'll never clear it."

"Sure, you will," said Robbie. "Remember, Wonder Kid can do anything."

Brian looked down again. He started to feel dizzy.

He closed his eyes and thought about being Wonder Kid. He wished that he were already dressed in the costume. Without it, it was hard to feel like a superhero.

"Hurry up," Robbie said. "We don't have all day!"

Brian braced himself and pushed off from the ladder. Even as he did so, he knew he was not going to make it across.

An instant later he felt his feet hit the hedge. Branches clawed at his body, and twigs scratched his face. Down, down, down he went into the very heart of the hedge. When at last he came to a stop, he felt as if he were being held in place by a million sticks jabbing into him from all directions.

After a moment, he slowly opened his eyes.

All he could see around him was a curtain of green.

9

"Brian?" Sarah's voice called anxiously. "Are you hurt?"

Brian tried to answer, but he could not make a sound. There didn't seem to be any air in his lungs.

"Brian?" Now it was Robbie's voice calling to him. "Are you okay?"

"Please, say something!" begged Lisa. "Tell us you're all right!" She sounded as if she was getting ready to cry.

Brian finally managed to draw in some breath.

"I don't know if I'm all right or not!" he shouted. "I'm stuck halfway down in the middle of the hedge."

"We'll get you out," Robbie said. "We have the hedge clippers. This side is so thick with leaves, though, that I think it might work best if I cut through from the other side."

"I'll go around and check it out," said Sarah. Brian could hear the pounding of her feet as she raced through the gate and out onto the playground.

After a moment, he heard some rustling and snapping. Then Sarah's hands appeared in front of his face. The hands tore at the leaves and branches until they had made a large enough hole so Sarah herself could peer in at him.

"You look funny," she said. "There's a leaf sticking out of your nose."

"I don't see anything funny about it," snapped Brian.

"Don't worry," said Sarah. "Robbie will get you out."

She drew her face back from the hole, and Brian glanced past her. What he saw caused him to gasp in horror.

A group of boys was striding toward them across the playground.

"Matt and his gang are coming!" Brian hissed at his sister.

Sarah whirled and jumped away from the hedge.

"Well, look who's here!" said Matt. "It's Wonder Kid's buddy! Where's Superhero today, still getting his teeth cleaned?"

"Wonder Kid will be a bit late," said Sarah. "He had to stop on his way to zap some bank robbers."

"Then it's lucky for you that you brought us lunch," said Matt. "Are those *two* sacks I see on the ground over there?"

"You wouldn't want to bother with those," said Sarah. "There's nothing in them but dry old peanut butter sandwiches."

"That's better than tuna," said Matt. "Isn't that right, guys?"

The boys in his gang burst out laughing, and Brian could hear the rustle of paper. He knew Matt was opening the sacks and unwrapping the sandwiches.

"Hey, great!" Matt exclaimed. "There's chocolate cake in this one!"

"You can't have that!" cried Sarah. "That cake is my brother's! He didn't eat any breakfast, and he'll be starved by lunchtime!"

Brian could not believe what he was hearing. He had never known Sarah to worry about someone else's stomach.

"Yum, yum!" said Matt, making smacking sounds with his lips. "Is there a piece of cake in that other sack too?"

"You're going to be sorry when Wonder Kid gets here!" cried Sarah.

"Don't be silly," said Matt. "You know there isn't any Wonder Kid. That kid in the funny costume was probably your brother. That creep's such a nerd, he could never stand up to anybody."

Brian was swept with a sudden surge of fury. He could not keep his mouth shut a moment longer.

"I'm on my way to Summerfield now!" he shouted. "If you bullies know what's good for you, you'll leave Sarah alone!"

For a moment Matt and his friends were too startled to speak.

Then one of the boys asked shakily, "Who was *that*?"

"That was Wonder Kid!" cried Sarah. "I told you he was coming! He's flying this way, and he's sending his voice ahead of him!"

"That's crazy," said Matt. "You can't project a voice without a phone or a radio."

"A superhero can!" Brian bellowed. "Superheroes have powerful vocal cords! You'd better get out of the way before the rest of me gets there!"

"We do need to hit the road, Matt," said one of the gang members. "If we don't get a move on, we're going to be late for school."

"Chicken!" sneered Matt. "You're nothing but a bunch of chickens! Can't you see this fat twerp is trying to trick us? I bet she has a radio stashed over there in the hedge."

"That wasn't a radio," another boy said. "That was really Wonder Kid talking. I recognized his voice."

"Somebody's cut a hole in the hedge," Matt insisted. "I'm going to look inside and see what's been hidden there."

Brian peered out through the opening in the hedge. He saw Matt coming toward him, and he felt like crying.

He thought about Matt's horrid face getting closer and closer.

He pictured Matt's mean eyes glaring in through the hole.

He decided that when that happened, he would spit in Matt's face. He only wished he still had a mouthful of cereal.

Then, all of a sudden, something astonishing happened. From somewhere above, a voice shouted, "*Look out below!*"

A figure came hurtling down from out of the sky. It was wearing a hood and a cape, and its arms bulged with muscles.

"*Wonder Kid to the rescue!*" cried the boy in the superhero outfit, and an instant later, he crashed right on top of Matt Gordon.

10

Suddenly a lot of voices were yelling at once.

There was so much noise and confusion that Brian couldn't tell exactly what was happening. Sarah had somehow managed to grab the lunch sacks and was waving them wildly about as if they were flags. She was also jumping up and down in front of the hole in the hedge, blocking Brian's view of everything but her back.

Then she hopped to one side, and he could see again.

On the far side of the playground, Matt's friends were racing away.

Brian had never seen boys run so fast.

Matt himself was lying flat on the ground, and standing over him was the powerful figure of Wonder Kid.

"So, you don't believe superheroes can fly?" he cried. "So, you don't believe they can project their voices and leap buildings? At least there's one thing you *have* to believe about superheroes: they always come to the rescue of their friends."

Matt made a whimpering noise like a frightened puppy.

"Please, don't zap me," he begged. "Oh, please don't zap me!"

"Then, repeat after me," said Wonder Kid: "*I believe in superheroes!*"

"I believe in superheroes," Matt responded quickly.

"I promise I will never snatch anybody's lunch again!"

Matt said, "I promise I'll never snatch anybody's lunch."

"And the Sixth-Grade Gate will be free to be used by everybody!"

"And the Sixth-Grade Gate — " Matt began. His voice broke. "Please don't zap me, Wonder Kid! I have very tender skin."

"Zap him!" Sarah commanded. "He called my brother a nerd!"

"What?" exclaimed Wonder Kid. "Matt called my friend a bad name?"

He raised his right arm into a zapping position.

"I take it back!" screamed Matt. "I didn't know Sarah's brother was a friend of yours! I'll never say anything mean about him again!"

"And the Sixth-Grade Gate?" prodded Wonder Kid.

"It will be free to be used by everybody!"

"All right," said the superhero. "I guess I can release you now."

"No, wait a minute!" cried Lisa, appearing out of nowhere. She was carrying a notebook in one hand and a camera in the other. "Before he gets up off the ground, I want to take a picture. I'll need it to illustrate my story for the newspaper."

She aimed the camera at Matt and Wonder Kid.

Wonder Kid pointed his finger as though he were zapping Matt.

Matt just lay in the dirt looking miserable and terrified.

"We'll have to print extra copies of this issue," said Lisa. "Everybody at school is going to want one."

"I'm letting you go now," Wonder Kid told Matt. "I want you to be sure, though, not to forget your promise: *You are never again to take away any kid's lunch*."

Matt jumped up off the ground and started

running. In a matter of seconds he had dis-
appeared into the school building.

As soon as Matt was out of sight, Wonder
Kid rushed to the hedge. He pulled off his
hood, and curly red hair sprang out.

"Did you see that wonderful leap I made?"
asked Robbie.

"That was only because you've got such
long legs," said Brian. He knew it was dumb
to be jealous, but he couldn't help it. "Your
aim was bad. You didn't come down in the
landing field."

"I couldn't see where it was," said Robbie.
"I had to take off my glasses. I knew Matt
would expect Wonder Kid to have perfect
eyesight."

Suddenly the sound of a bell rang out across
the playground.

"Oh, no!" cried Sarah. "We're going to be
late again!"

"You girls go ahead," said Robbie. "I'll
stay here and get Brian out."

"We'll all stay," said Lisa. "If we're late, we're late together."

She went back to the sidewalk and returned with the pair of hedge clippers. Within a short time Robbie had widened Sarah's hole enough so Brian could scramble through.

Lisa's eyes widened with horror at the sight of his scratches.

"Do they hurt a lot?" she asked anxiously.

"Not really," said Brian. "My skin must be tougher than Matt's." Then he heard himself saying something that surprised him as much as anyone. "You know, I'm actually going to miss being Wonder Kid. Whenever I put on that costume, I stopped feeling like a nerd."

"You shouldn't *ever* feel like a nerd!" exclaimed Robbie. "After all, you're the one who *invented* Wonder Kid! And he doesn't have to be gone for good, you know. We can always bring him back when there are people who need him."

"We can all take turns being Wonder Kid," said Lisa. "There's no good reason superheroes have to be boys."

"As long as we don't get too fat for the costume," said Brian. At that, everybody turned to look at Sarah.

"Let's vote," said Lisa. "Everybody in favor of keeping Wonder Kid, raise your hand."

The vote came out four to zero in favor of keeping him.

Sarah licked chocolate frosting off her fingers.

"Once a friend, always a friend," she said.